To Kim and Thom

First edition 2010

Library of Congress Cataloging-in-Publication Data
Cowen-Fletcher, Jane.
Hello, Puppy! / Jane Cowen-Fletcher.—1st ed.
p. cm.
Summary: A child spends time with her new puppy,
learning what it means when puppy yawns, stretches, and sniffs.
ISBN 978-0-7636-4303-4
[1. Dogs—Fiction. 2. Animals—Infancy—Fiction.] I. Title. II. Title: Hello, Puppy!
PZ7.C8365Whd 2010
[E]—dc22   2008044133

10 11 12 13 14 15 LEO 10 9 8 7 6 5 4 3 2 1

Printed in Heshan, Guangdong, China

This book was typeset in Clichee.
The illustrations were done in pastel.

Candlewick Press
99 Dover Street
Somerville, Massachusetts 02144

visit us at www.candlewick.com

Hello, Puppy!

Jane Cowen-Fletcher

CANDLEWICK PRESS

What's that puppy doing?

She's sleeping.
Puppies need lots of sleep.

Now she's waking up.

"Hello, Puppy!"

What's that puppy doing now?

She's stre-e-etching . . .

and giving herself a good shake!

What's that puppy looking for?

She's looking for something to eat.
She must be hungry.

Why is that puppy sniff, sniff, sniffing all around?

Oops! That means she needs to go potty . . . outside!

"What a smart puppy!"

Now what is that puppy doing?

She's running with me,

and playing with me,

and giving me puppy kisses.

"I love you, Puppy!"